The
Medium

Also by Linda Westphal

The Hermit Bookstore

The

Medium

a short story

Linda Westphal

LindaWestphal.com

The Medium

For the reader who has lost someone they love

The

Medium

Dear Reader,

This short story is best enjoyed in a quiet place where your mind can relax and indulge in the meditative experience of reading.

LW

When tragedy visits you and delivers something unimaginable, the circumstances have a way of opening your heart and soul like you can't imagine. I know this to be true because eight months ago tragedy visited me.

On this Thursday afternoon in October, the air outside unusually crisp and still, I'm sitting on a plum-colored velvet sofa in Savannah's historic district.

While the exterior of the building has not changed in over 160 years, the interior has been remodeled and office suites now occupy the rooms.

A delicate scent (rose?) dances in my direction more than once as I take in the details of Caroline's office, which had once been the home's library. Decorated in a traditional Southern style, the room is as comforting as a big warm Southern hug. Even so, I'm a bundle of nerves about being here—in the office of a medium.

Caroline is not a stranger to me. A mutual friend formally introduced us in 2008, and over the years we've been invited to many of the same Savannah dinner parties. She is highly admired and respected in Savannah (as well as all over the world, I hear) for her ability to communicate with those who have passed on. Yet I've never felt inclined, until recently, to seek her assistance.

My hands in my lap are shaking. I take a slow, deep breath in and let it out even slower, forcing myself to relax. *What if no one comes forward to speak to me today?* I wonder. It is certainly possible. I close my eyes and focus on my breathing and the floral scent that hangs in the room. A moment later I hear the distant sound of heels hitting the wooden floor. I listen, my eyes still closed, as the sound gets closer and closer to the room where I am sitting.

When I hear the tall, wooden French doors open, I look in their direction and watch Caroline enter, her heels still clapping against the floor.

"Hello, Lacy," she says, her face gentle and her eyes wide and bright. She stops for a brief second and holds my gaze. All I can do is give her a weary smile. "Thank you for waiting." She turns and closes the doors, then settles in the Queen Anne chair next to the velvet sofa where I'm sitting. "Don't be afraid," she says. "All is well."

I brush an imaginary wisp of hair off my forehead and try to say something, anything, but nothing comes out. Again, I tell myself to relax, to trust Caroline and enjoy the experience.

She picks up a brilliant rough-cut purple amethyst from the table next to her chair and warms it in her hand. "Is this your first experience with a medium?" she asks.

I nod and manage to answer, "Yes."

"Please don't give me any details about why you're here. Spirit will guide us and provide what you need."

Then she closes her eyes and appears to be using energy from the amethyst to tap into wherever she goes to hear messages from the other side.

A few minutes later she opens her eyes and says, "A young male spirit is here with us. He looks to be in his midthirties, and has dark hair, brown eyes, and an athletic build." She pauses. "He says his name is Daniel."

My heart races and I gasp. "My husband."

"Was it difficult for you to come today?"

Caroline asks.

"Yes," I say softly, unable to look her in the eyes.

"Daniel just told me it took a lot of courage for you to come today. He's glad you're here."

I want to hold it together, but Caroline's words hit a nerve and tears well up. She hands me a box of tissues, and my words come tumbling out. "I didn't lose only a husband. I also lost our dreams, our future plans, and my idea of myself in those dreams and plans. No matter how hard I try, I can't see anything in my life beyond today and that frightens me. There's so much love around Harry and me, and I'm truly grateful for the kindness of our friends, but their looks of pity and relief that it's my bad fortune and not theirs only makes it worse."

"Daniel says you're doing fine. He'll be with you whenever you need him. He wants you to live the full, beautiful life you deserve. He also wants to thank you for keeping his memory alive with your son. He was there with you at his birthday party—right beside you the whole time."

Harry's fifth birthday party was two weeks ago at Daniel's parents' house, just a few blocks from here. I sensed Daniel that day, but I brushed it off and now I'm sorry.

"He says he wouldn't have missed Harry's reaction when he saw the puppy for anything." She laughs. "He's pretty proud of himself—taking credit for the idea."

Then I laugh. "Yes, he was right. The day he died we talked about getting Harry a dog. I thought Harry was too young. Daniel vehemently disagreed."

"Daniel says he's sorry for being careless with his life. It was an accident. He was driving too fast . . . couldn't handle the curve in the road." She pauses. "He died instantly."

I blow my nose into a tissue.

"Daniel's energy is pulling back," Caroline says.

"No! Can he stay a little longer?"

"Daniel hasn't been on the other side very long. His soul is still adjusting. It takes a lot of energy to communicate with those who are earthbound."

Caroline is looking at me as she explains this. Then her eyes move to something behind me, over my right shoulder.

"He has one last request."

"What is it?" I dab my nose with a tissue.

"He wants me to introduce you to your spirit guide."

Caroline's eyes are now fixed on me.

"It's an unusual request," she says, "but I think he's right. Your guide can help you heal and move on." She sets the amethyst on the table beside her. "I can help you connect to your spirit guide through hypnosis. Have you ever been hypnotized?"

"No," I say, feeling calmer now that I know Daniel is all right.

"Everyone has what I call a spirit guide," Caroline says. "Your spirit guide's purpose, from the day you are born, is to help you with your life's mission and keep you on the right track." She lightly taps my knee. "Close your eyes, dear. Relax. Think about the happiest moment in your life."

I rest my head on the back of the sofa and close my eyes.

"Tell me about your happiest moment," Caroline says. "Who are you with?"

"I'm with Daniel and Harry on an airplane. It's our first trip together. Harry's thirteen months old." I giggle. "The flight attendant is pinning wings on his shirt."

"You're doing just fine," Caroline says, her voice helping me relax even more. "Now go back farther in time—when you were Harry's age. What do you see?"

As if on command my mind leaps back, and I see myself peering out a large window at hills of snow that had fallen during the night. The snow blocks the front door and threatens to block my view out the window. "I see a lot of snow."

"You're doing very well. Now go back even farther—before your birth. Tell me what you see."

"I'm on a beach . . . sitting in an Adirondack chair . . . looking at the ocean. Someone's walking toward me. It's a woman. I don't recognize her, but I feel as if I know her. She's beautiful . . . tall, with straight, long black hair, dark eyes."

Caroline gently touches my arm. "She's your spirit guide. Ask her to tell you her name."

The beautiful woman sits in the sand in front of my chair, looks at me, and smiles. In my mind I ask, "What's your name?"

Her response fills my head. That's when I realize we are communicating through telepathy. "Ria," she says with a slight Spanish accent.

"Are you my spirit guide?" I ask.

"Yes. We have known each other for many lifetimes. I am here to help you in this lifetime."

I feel an overwhelming rush of warmth, like love, run through my body. "I've seen you in my dreams," I whisper.

Ria grins. "It's the only place you listen to my words, Lacy. You refuse to hear me when you're awake. You must pay attention and watch for signs of help from the other side. Trust your instincts when they tell you a sign is for you. You need to use this basic human sense to help you accomplish your mission in this lifetime."

I gasp and hold my breath for an instant as I process her words. *My life isn't over after all.*

"Lacy, don't worry about your future. Take one day at a time and follow your heart. Spend time alone—get to know yourself. This will bring the peace and guidance you need now."

Ria continues. "The sorrow you feel when you think of Daniel's death will always be with you, but over time your sadness will change to deep love and understanding. You will never forget him, nor should you.

"One day you'll realize why his early passing was destined to change your life, and Harry's. You will also see how much you've grown because of it. You will accomplish great things in the years ahead, Lacy, and bring happiness to many people you don't know."

"But Ria, how do I create a new life? Except for Harry, I lost everything when Daniel died." I'm trembling.

"Your soul already knows what to do, Lacy. You came into this lifetime knowing. Don't worry— you have it in you to begin again. And the people you know and love on this side will be right behind you, helping you when you need it."

I can't hold it anymore and I begin to sob, finally releasing all the emotions I've held inside for the past eight months. I am relieved to know that my life isn't over. *There's an important reason for me to be alive. I do have a future.*

Ria stands and kisses my cheek. "I'm always

with you, Lacy, even when your fear or doubt is so strong it cuts off your ability to sense me. Nothing in your life happens by accident. Every act, meeting, argument, lucky break—everything—is meant to help you move forward or help you through a challenge." She smiles. "All is well, dear Lacy, all is well."

And then she's gone, and I'm alone again on the beach. A few minutes pass and I hear Caroline's voice pulling me back to Savannah. I slowly open my eyes and see her sitting in the Queen Anne chair. "Was she able to help you?" she asks.

I lean forward and pull another tissue from the box on the table, then wipe my eyes. "Ria said Daniel's death was meant to happen at this time. And I will be able to create a new life for Harry and me." At that moment I feel a remarkable sense of newness, a new beginning, as if I can hardly wait for my future to reveal itself. I thank Caroline for her help and kiss her good-bye.

As I walk into the cool October day, the world feels different—more alive. I sense the age of the cobblestones under my feet. The giant oak trees that filter the sun from my face appear strong, wise. The fallen leaves rattle and tumble around me, reminding me of the changing seasons and how much life resembles nature. But best of all, I've finally given myself permission to keep going. Even though I don't know what my future holds, my fear of it has been replaced with wonder about the new life I will be creating. "All is well," I say out loud. "All is well, indeed."

Excerpt from *The Hermit Bookstore*

The Hermit Bookstore
Copyright © 2015 by Linda Westphal

Mary June
Wednesday, April 23, 2014, morning

A fine misty rain fell on the small northern California town of Lotus as Mary June Shaw jogged the curves of Lotus Road. She had considered blaming the seasonal mix of dewy clouds and early morning sunlight outside her bedroom window for her inability to sleep, but her instincts hinted at something else—something important she had to do today. Whatever it was, it had coaxed her out of bed at dawn on her day off as marketing director at Rivers Winery.

Lotus, population 295, had not always been a small, quiet town. More than 165 years ago, when gold was discovered here, the nearby American River was overrun within a few months by men from all over the world who dreamed of finding their fortunes.

Mary June slowed her pace, took in the view, and wondered what her little town may have been like during the California gold rush. She imagined makeshift camps along the river that offered the essentials—a doctor, a blacksmith, a sleeping lodge, a food kitchen, a tavern, mail services, and other services a man was willing to trade for a little gold. Surely, she thought, the scene was nothing like today's quiet picturesque destination that was abandoned most of the year, except in the summer when families and groups dropped in for the thrill of whitewater rafting on the river.

Her gait changed to a fast walk as she approached the Uniontown Cemetery and focused on her breathing—in and out, in and out, in and out. In the distance she could see the tiny old brick post office, built in 1881, and just beyond it a farmhouse about the same age.

It wasn't until she reached the front of the old post office that she saw a light in the downstairs window of the farmhouse—a house that was supposed to be vacant. She stood still, barely breathing, and narrowed her eyes to get a better look. "Oh my God," she whispered. Her heart pounded in her chest. *Someone's in the house!*

Mary June crossed the street and approached cautiously, taking a second look at a large wooden sign hanging from a post in front of the house. She was sure it had not been there yesterday. Then she noticed the For Sale sign that had been posted at the edge of the yard, near the road, was gone.

She shifted her weight to her right leg and leaned forward until she could see the front of the new sign, which hung from two large metal hooks that were attached to a wooden post. She read the words carved into the wood—The Hermit Bookstore. A carved drawing next to the name featured a cloaked man with a brightly lit lantern in one hand and a walking stick in the other.

She walked up to the farmhouse and through a side window saw an older woman, dressed in a long rainbow-patterned skirt and a loose white blouse, placing books on a bookshelf that stood higher than her five-foot frame. She watched the woman for a few minutes, then moved toward the front of the house, walked up the stairs, and crossed the front porch. Without thinking, she knocked on the door.

Before she finished knocking, the woman she had been watching—with her hippie-like clothes, long blonde wavy hair, and sparkling blue eyes that reminded Mary June of the American River on a bright sunny day—opened the door.

"Hello! You're my first customer today," said

the stranger on the other side of the threshold. She held the door open for Mary June.

It took Mary June a moment to react. The scene behind the woman was not what she had expected. On the floor, running down the middle of the parlor, lay a faded Persian rug with various shades of gold that matched the honey-colored oak floor and wood trim. The welcoming sight pulled her eyes a good twenty feet into the room to a round antique table full of books at the opposite end of the rug. Mary June's nose twitched as she caught a whiff of sweet lilacs, old books, and worn furniture. "Umm, hi," she finally managed to say.

She thought she heard the woman giggle softly in her throat, but the mature face looking back at her only offered a pleasant smile. As she studied the stranger's face (her shockingly-white skin and crow's-feet just starting to form at the corners of her eyes), she could not recall if they had ever met. The woman was a stranger but she didn't feel like a stranger. Mary June wasn't at all uncomfortable when the woman caught and held her gaze for a long minute, as if she was looking inside her, watching her life's story.

"This is Feather," the woman said, breaking the connection and referring to the furry-faced, butt-wagging mutt at her feet. "And I'm Jolene. Jolene Fields. Welcome to The Hermit Bookstore." She

opened the door wider and attached a hook on the
door to an eye latch on the wall.

Mary June's feet remained planted on the
front porch, her upper body stretched halfway in the
door. She looked wide-eyed at the old farmhouse
parlor and the room beyond it, which was once the
dining room. Tall, wooden bookshelves stood like
soldiers in vertical rows to the left and right of the
Persian rug, and a creamy white marble fireplace
stood against the wall on her right.

She had never seen the farmhouse look so
good; somehow, it looked fifty years younger. The
floors, polished back to life, glowed as sunlight from
the windows hit the planks. The matching oak
molding throughout the two rooms appeared almost
new. The farmhouse had been transformed into a
fabulous bookstore with row after row of six-foot-
high shelves packed with books. The only thing out of
place was a small box of unpacked books in front of a
shelf where Jolene was standing.

Less than twenty-four hours ago the building
had been a cold, abandoned farmhouse. But now,
with its warm and inviting atmosphere, a person
might think it had been there for years. It hardly
seemed possible that someone could pull it together
so quickly, and without any gossip about it at Sutter
Diner.

"Come on in, darlin'. Look around if you'd like."

Mary June watched Jolene pull books from the box and place them on the shelf marked History. "Did the owners sell the farmhouse?" she asked, stepping inside the room.

"I'm just renting it temporarily."

Mary June frowned, wondering why anyone would go to so much trouble for a temporary bookstore. The thought faded away as soon as she reached the round antique table at the end of the rug. A small metal sign that read Shopkeeper's Monthly Picks sat on top of a stack of books. She walked slowly around the table, scanning the book titles. The books included a mix of adult and children's classics, a few New York Times bestsellers, and a number of titles she didn't recognize. One book in particular stood out—a hardcover novel with a plantation house and live oak trees on the front cover.

"Can I help you find something?"

Startled, Mary June looked up to see Jolene's kind, blue eyes. Jolene caught and held her gaze again, then turned and appeared to be searching for a book on the shelf behind her.

"What do you like to read? Fiction or

nonfiction?" Jolene asked, finally pulling the book she was looking for from the shelf.

"This looks interesting," Mary June said. She turned the book in her hand so Jolene could see the front cover.

"Well, bless your heart. Are you a Southern girl, too?"

Mary June blushed and averted her eyes. "I was."

"My dear, once a Southern girl, always a Southern girl."

Mary June nodded and smiled. She may have left rural Georgia more than nine years ago, but she still felt like a Southern girl at heart.

"Where's your family from, dear?" Jolene asked.

"Mama's family is from Alabama, Daddy's from Mississippi."

"Yes indeed. You come from good Southern roots. When did you come to California, sugar?"

Mary June hesitated. She wasn't sure she wanted to talk to a stranger about her troubled family history. "I've been here awhile." Turning her shoulder as she pulled her attention back to the table, she hoped Jolene would get the hint that she had shared enough.

"Here, take this." Jolene held up the book Mary June had seen her take from the shelf. "Consider it a gift from one Southern girl to another." Her eyes smiled.

Mary June took the book and read the title— *Travels with Charley*. It sounded somewhat familiar. Then she noticed the author's name, John Steinbeck. *Of course*, she thought, *the author of* Of Mice and Men *and* The Grapes of Wrath.

"Thank you," she said, giving Jolene a grateful smile. "How much do I owe you for this one?" She held up the Southern novel she had found on the table.

Jolene checked the back cover. "Six dollars and fifty cents should cover it. Would you like a bag for your books?"

"No. I live around the corner. I can carry them." Mary June pulled a ten-dollar bill from the zippered pocket of her jogging jacket and handed it to Jolene.

Jolene rang up the sale and returned the change. "I'm glad you stopped by to say hello, Mary

June." Jolene stared purposefully as she spoke. "Come back soon and let me know what you think of Steinbeck's book."

As Mary June walked to her apartment, replaying the strange encounter with Jolene in her mind, she wondered if the bookstore was the reason she couldn't sleep this morning. How did Jolene know she was at the front door? How did she know her name? Mary June had never mentioned her name. And what about that book? Jolene had intentionally pulled *Travels with Charley* from the shelf for her. However strange the experience had been, it didn't feel creepy. In fact, it felt good, perhaps even . . . necessary. Maybe things would make sense when she started reading it. She picked up her pace and didn't slow until she reached her apartment.

Mario
Wednesday, April 23, 2014

The morning sun had tried to force its way through the window blinds of the law office reception area about an hour ago, but Mario Pico didn't bother getting up to let it in. He liked to work in the dark with only the banker's light on his desk illuminating the room. He had picked up this habit in law school, where he did his best work at night when it was quiet and he was alone.

Mario leaned all the way back in the leather chair at his desk and stretched his arms, causing his fingertips to tap the window blinds behind him. This made him think of the many strained conversations he had had with his secretary, Tracey, about the blinds. She didn't think it mattered if they were closed at night, but to him it was a big deal because he usually arrived and left when it was dark. The mere suggestion that someone could be watching him from the other side of a dark window spooked him, and made it impossible for him to concentrate on his work. He also worried about the contents of the office, not wanting to tempt thieves who may be lurking around the neighborhood. "Just close them when you leave; it solves a number of issues," he reminded Tracey at least once a week. Her usual response was an eye roll and the line, "What would I do if I didn't have you to remind me?"

His thoughts drifted to the number of hours he worked and his less-than-perfect love life. At his thirtieth birthday party last week, he had done a pretty good job of deflecting the hazing from his friends about showing up without a date, but he knew what they said was true. Last year he wanted to give Katie what she wanted—marriage—but he didn't feel ready for it. In retrospect, he didn't blame her for wanting to end the relationship. In fact her ability to move forward once she had made a decision about what she wanted was one of the characteristics he had admired most about her.

He shook off the chatter in his head and sat up in the chair. It was still early, just after eight in the morning. Tracey would be in soon. He opened his calendar on his laptop. Except for a court appearance in Sacramento at 3:30 p.m., his day was clear. He reached for a large file on the table next to his desk and began reviewing his notes.

About eleven, he closed the file and reached for his suit jacket that hung on the coat rack near the door.

"I'm going out for a while," he said to Tracey, who sat at her desk in the reception area. "Can I get you anything?"

"I know it's hard to believe, but"—she gazed up at him sheepishly from the top of her reading glasses—"I didn't have time this morning to pack a lunch. If it's not too much trouble, I'd love a turkey Lunch Box from Sutter Diner."

"You got it." He reached for the door and closed it behind him.

It was too early for lunch, so he decided to take a ride around the curves of Highway 49. When he felt restless, he drove. Anywhere. Driving helped him think.

To continue reading, order THE HERMIT BOOKSTORE at LindaWestphal.com

About the Author

Linda Westphal has written professionally since 1990 and now spends most of her time writing stories. *The Medium* is her first work of fiction. Her second book, *The Hermit Bookstore*, is available wherever books are sold. Linda lives in Northern California.

Connect with Linda Westphal —

Subscribe to receive updates and details about giveaways at **LindaWestphal.com**

Twitter: @Author_Westphal